For Sam

First published 2013 by Macmillan Children's Books
This edition published 2014 by Macmillan Children's Books
a division of Macmillan Publishers Limited
20 New Wharf Road, London, N1 9RR
Basingstoke and Oxford
Associated companies throughout the world
www.panmacmillan.com

ISBN: 978-1-4472-4236-9

3 5 7 9 8 6 4 2

A CIP catalogue record for this book is available from the British Library.

Printed in Belgium

Aunt
Amelia

Rebecca Cobb

MACMILLAN CHILDREN'S BOOKS

We were in a bad mood.

Aunt Amelia was coming to look after us.

We didn't know who Aunt Amelia

was and we didn't want looking after.

Dad said we had met her once when we were tiny.

Mum said we had to be good.

Mum and Dad left a list of instructions.
"Thank you," said Aunt Amelia, "I'm sure
these will be very useful."

We started on the list straight away.
It said . . .

Please tell the children to be careful if you go to the park.

Don't let them go near the edge of the pond . . .

or get themselves too dirty.

They can have an ice-cream, but just one each.

They already have plenty of toys . . .

and don't let them pester you for sweets.

The children will need some quiet time

so they don't get over-excited.

Make sure that they help you with keeping the house clean . . .

and tidy . . .

and neat.

For dinner, they can choose what to have
as long as it is something sensible.

They are allowed one story before bedtime . . .

but absolutely no television . . .

and don't let them stay up too late.

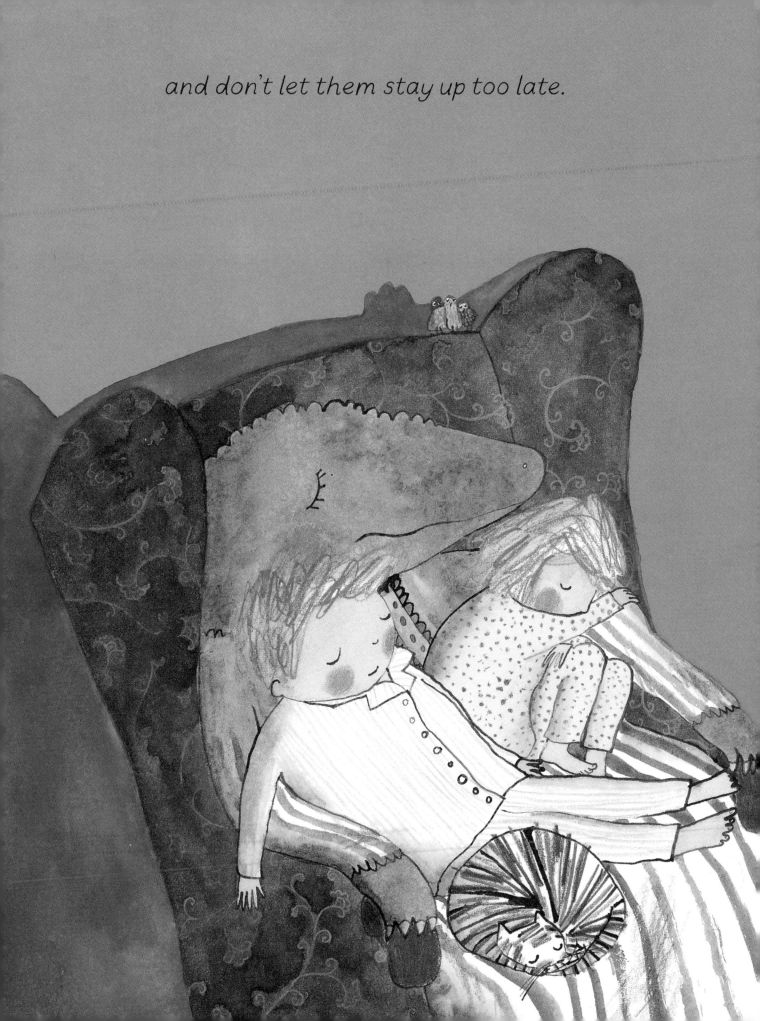

The next day Mum and Dad were coming home,

so we got the house ready for them.

"I hope they've been good?" asked Mum.

"Good as gold," said Aunt Amelia.

"Were the instructions helpful?" asked Dad.

"Very," said Aunt Amelia.

Mum and Dad asked if we would
like Aunt Amelia to come and look
after us again sometime.

"Yes, please!" we said.
"And perhaps you
could write another list!"